MEDICAL TECHNOLOGY

INSPIRED BY NATURE

by Venessa Bellido Schwarz

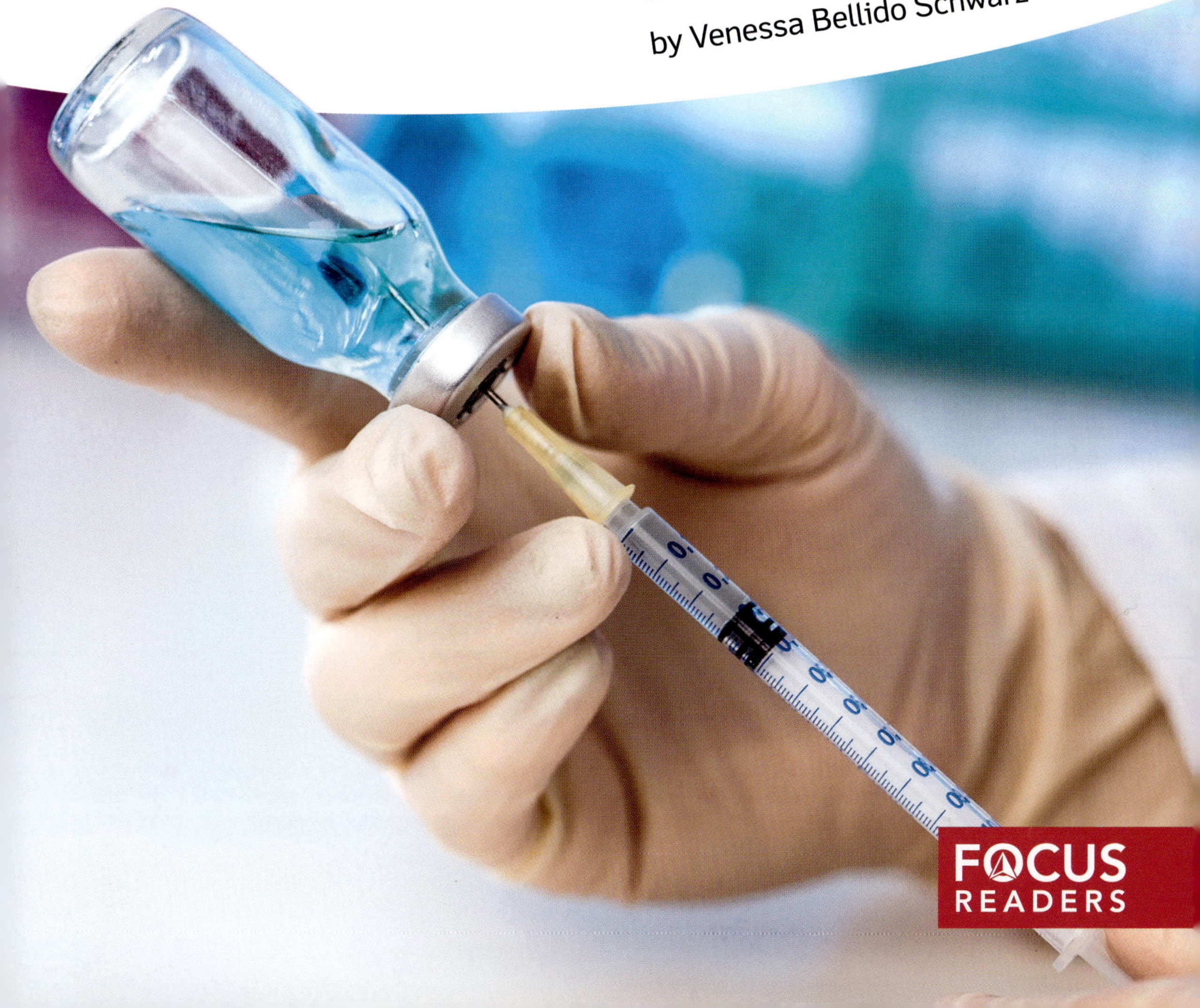

FOCUS READERS

FOCUS READERS

WWW.FOCUSREADERS.COM

Focus Readers is distributed by North Star Editions:
sales@northstareditions.com | 888-417-0195

Produced for Focus Readers by Red Line Editorial.

Content Consultant: Russell J. Stewart, Professor of Bioengineering, University of Utah

Photographs ©: Adfoto/Shutterstock Images, cover, 1; DDCoral/Shutterstock Images, 4–5; Red Line Editorial, 6; Jaco Bothma Empire Photo/Shutterstock Images, 9; Sucha Kittiwararat/Shutterstock Images, 10–11; Shamleen/Shutterstock Images, 12–13; Karplab, 15, 28; H.Tanaka/Shutterstock Images, 17; Gregory A. Pozhvanov/Shutterstock Images, 18–19; 3Dstock/Shutterstock Images, 21; REDPIXEL.PL/Shutterstock Images, 23; divedog/Shutterstock Images, 24–25; teekayu/Shutterstock Images, 27

ISBN
978-1-63517-942-2 (hardcover)
978-1-64185-044-5 (paperback)
978-1-64185-246-3 (ebook pdf)
978-1-64185-145-9 (hosted ebook)

Library of Congress Control Number: 2018931311

Printed in the United States of America
Mankato, MN
May, 2018

ABOUT THE AUTHOR

Venessa Bellido Schwarz has been published in several children's magazines. Her short story was on display with the Smithsonian Institution's Traveling Waterway Exhibition, and she was on the application committee for the 2018 WeNeedDiverseBooks mentorship program.

TABLE OF CONTENTS

CHAPTER 1

ANIMAL-INSPIRED GLUE

Scientists are inventing new medical technology. They are interested in biomimicry. Biomimicry is the science of copying nature to solve human problems. For example, one invention was inspired by the gecko. This sticky-footed lizard can climb walls and ceilings. It has tiny hairs on its feet that help it cling to surfaces.

Geckos can scale smooth vertical surfaces.

Scientists wanted to make an invention that could do the same.

In 2008, one scientist invented a new type of surgical tape. The tape's surface is similar to a gecko's feet. The tape can help people who are injured. It

THE GECKO FOOT

The hairs on a gecko's foot are flexible. They bend in order to make close contact with surfaces.

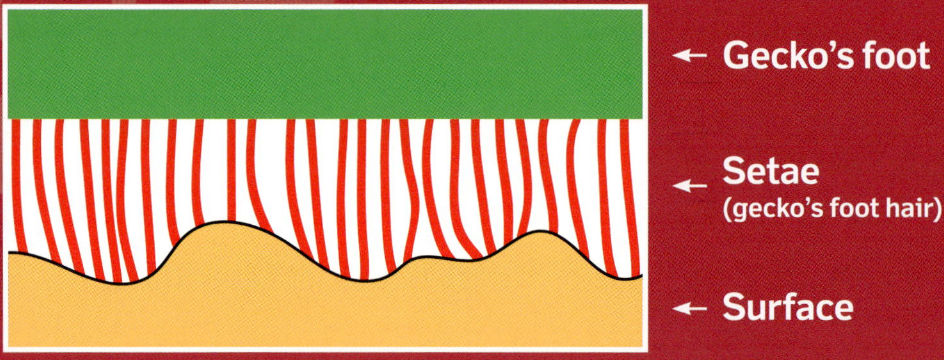

bonds patients' wounds. The tape holds the wounds together so they can heal. Afterward, the tape comes off with ease.

One year later, the creator of the tape received a letter from a doctor at Boston Children's Hospital. The doctor worked with patients who had heart defects. He was struggling to seal holes in his patients' hearts. He needed glue stronger than the "gecko" tape.

Inventing this type of glue would be a challenge. The human heart is soaked with blood. It also moves forcefully as it pumps. But the scientist who received the letter was determined. Before long, he learned about the sandcastle worm.

This worm creates a sticky substance. The worm uses the substance to glue sand and seashells together underwater. The scientist and his team came up with an idea from it. They created a glue that repels water. The glue would soak into the heart and create a waterproof seal.

LIFE-CHANGING TAPE

Doctors have used gecko-inspired tapes since 2001. But the "gecko" tape invented in 2008 is different. As the tape breaks down, it puts medicine into the patient's body. It also causes less swelling than other tapes. When it is used on the skin, the tape comes off with ease. But when it is used inside the body, it dissolves into the bloodstream.

Sandcastle worms use their natural glue to make tube-shaped homes.

In 2016, four hospitals in France tested the glue. They tried to seal holes in the hearts of 36 patients. The glue worked well on the patients' beating hearts. The scientists' new invention was a success.

IVY INSPIRATION

Ivy plants stick to the sides of buildings. The plants' roots dig into tiny cracks in the wall. Then they release a glue-like substance. The glue helps the plant hold on to the wall. As the ivy grows, it spreads in different directions.

The surgical glue inspired by the sandcastle worm works similarly. The glue seeps into the tiny cracks of an organ. Then it spreads in different directions. However, scientists struggled to hold the glue in place.

To fix the problem, the scientists invented a device that looks like a pen. The pen lets off a ray of light. This light makes the glue stay in place. The process takes less than five seconds.

Ivy plants can cover entire buildings using their glue-like substance.

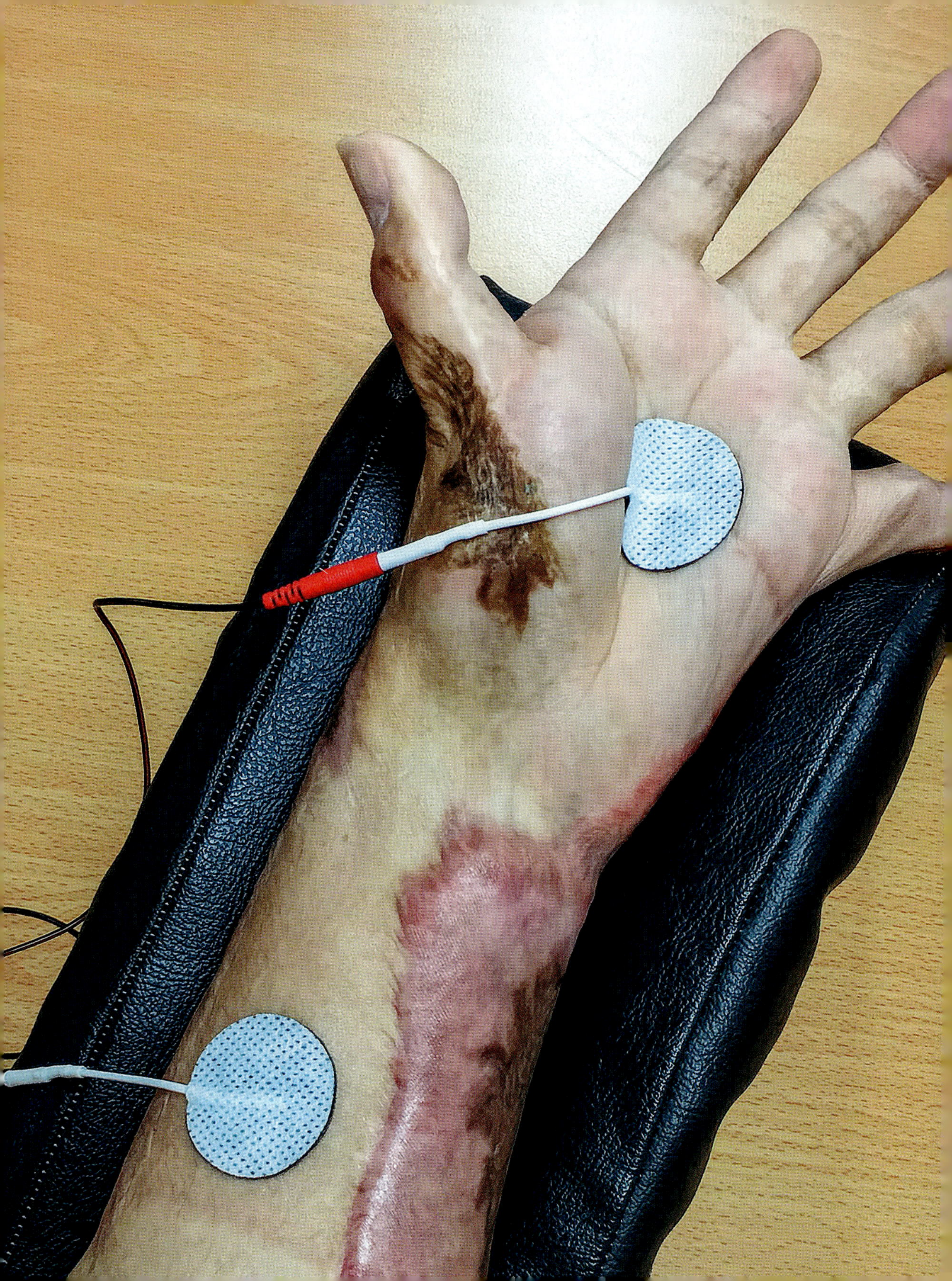

CHAPTER 2

TREATING INJURY AND DISEASE

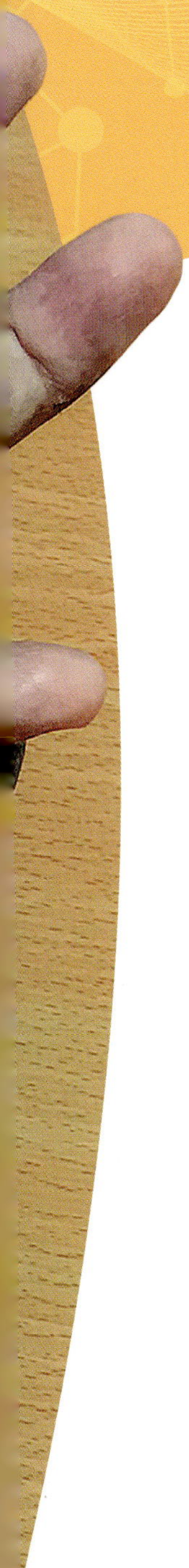

Some nature-inspired inventions help patients with injuries. In 2013, for example, scientists studied nature to help burn victims. For many years, doctors have done a surgery called a skin graft. They take healthy skin **tissue** from other places on the patient's body. They use it to replace the damaged skin.

Skin grafts can change in color. This makes the area lighter or darker than the surrounding skin.

To improve skin grafts, scientists turned to flesh-grabbing worms. One type of worm uses its sharp spine to pierce its prey's flesh. Then it inflates its spiny head inside the tissue. This process helps the worm latch on.

Scientists used the worm as a model for a new type of skin graft. In the

A DESIGN FOR MANY USES

Doctors perform skin grafts for a variety of patients. Skin grafting can help treat skin infections and large wounds. It can also help treat skin cancer. This makes the worm-inspired skin graft all the more important. These skin grafts are three times stronger than other materials used in the past.

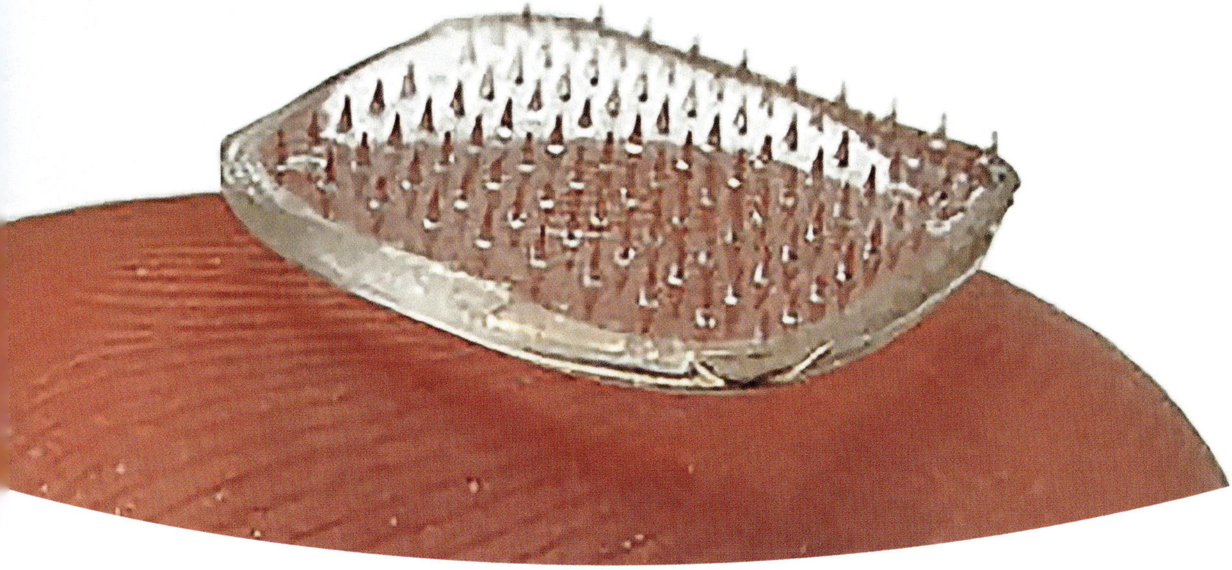

Scientists tested the needle patch on raw chicken and pig skin.

improved process, doctors pierce burned skin with a patch of tiny needles. Similar to the worm's head, the tips of the needles inflate. They keep the healthy skin in place while the burned tissue heals.

Nature-inspired technology has also helped doctors treat certain diseases.

One example is a **microchip** designed for cancer patients. Scientists based this idea on jellyfish. These sea creatures use their long tentacles to catch food. They can extend their tentacles far away from their bodies. This helps them grab food from a distance.

In 2012, scientists created a microchip that would help them do something similar. The scientists combined strands of **DNA** to create a long, wispy material. One end of the material is attached to the microchip. The other end reaches into the patient's bloodstream. The strand grabs **cancer cells** and counts them. This cell count is very helpful to doctors. It lets

The tentacles of a large box jellyfish can reach up to 10 feet (3.0 m) in length.

them know whether or not the patient's medicine is working.

The new microchip can count cells 10 times faster than previous devices. This makes a great difference. Doctors can more quickly determine which medicines to use. They can also decide on the right amounts. As a result, patients are more likely to recover.

CHAPTER 3

NATURE'S MEDICINE

People have turned to nature to treat illnesses for thousands of years. Some medicines are made from plants. And scientists continue to discover new ways that plants can be helpful. For example, a rare flower might help treat Alzheimer's disease. Patients with this disease slowly lose their memory and thinking skills.

Medicine made from the flower *Galanthus caucasicus* may improve patients' memory.

Scientists still haven't found a cure for Alzheimer's disease. But the flower's bulb makes a **compound** that can slow down the disease.

Using the flower as medicine would be expensive. It could also cause the flower to go **extinct**. So instead, scientists made a copy. To do so, they created a new chemical compound. It was similar to the flower's compound. And it had the same effect on the disease. This helped protect the rare flower. It also lowered the cost of making the medicine.

Scientists find ideas for medicine from animals, too. One example is a **vaccine** inspired by tardigrades. Tardigrades

Tardigrades are also known as water bears.

are eight-legged water animals. They're so small they can be seen only with a microscope. These tiny animals have amazing abilities. When tardigrades dry out, they become **dormant**. But water can make them active again. They can be revived even after 100 years.

Tardigrades can also survive harsh conditions. They coat their cells with a type of sugar. The sugar protects the animal's cells. This helps them survive after being dried out for decades.

TREATING HIGH BLOOD PRESSURE

The jararaca is a snake found in South America. One bite from the snake can kill a human. The snake's venom causes the person's blood pressure to fall quickly. Scientists invented a chemical compound similar to the snake's venom. Now, doctors are using the compound to treat high blood pressure. Left untreated, high blood pressure can cause heart attacks. The snake-inspired medicine keeps blood pressure at a safe level.

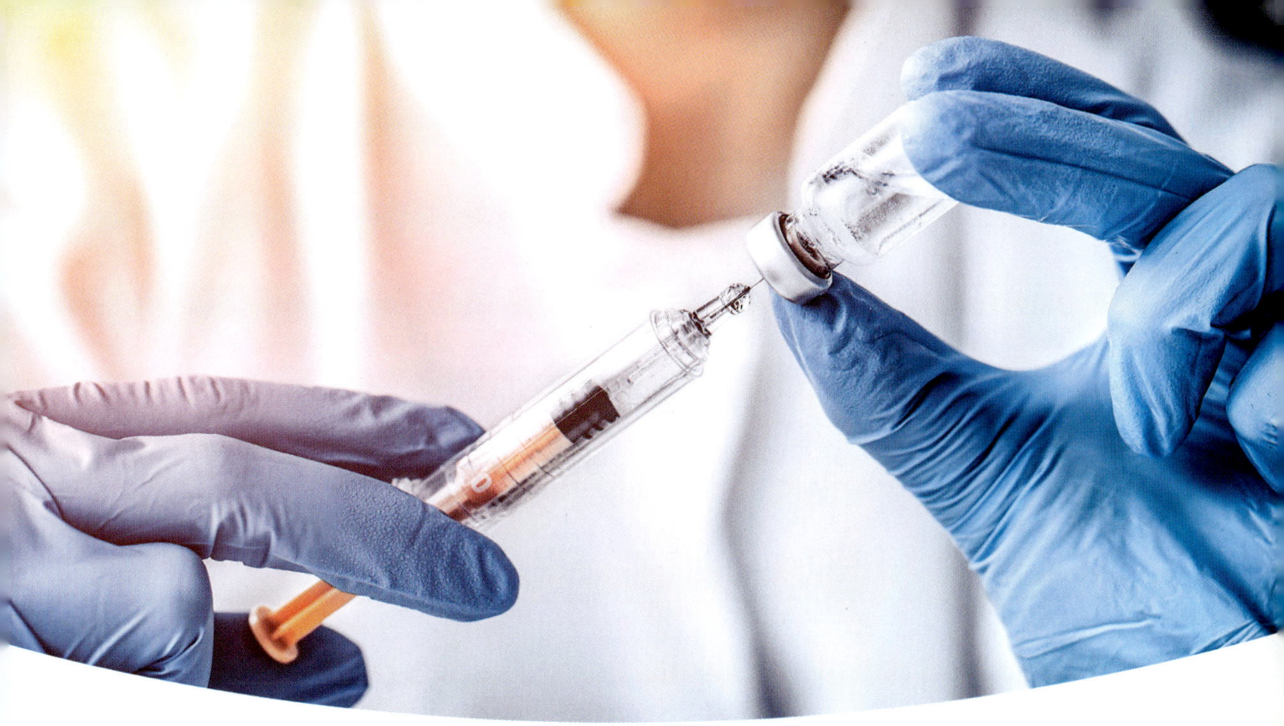

The tardigrade-inspired sugar coating allows more people to receive vaccines.

Tardigrades inspired scientists to create a sugar-coated vaccine. Like other medicines, vaccines can **expire**. Most need to be kept in cold temperatures. The sugar coating helps the vaccine last longer. It can go without refrigeration for up to six months. This way, the vaccine can be shipped across the world.

CHAPTER 4

FUTURE INSPIRATION

Inventing new medical technology takes years. The inventions must go through lots of testing. Scientists are working on many projects. One medical technology that is now in the works was inspired by seaweed. When seaweed is dry, it shrinks. But when it's wet, it expands.

Wet seaweed has long, ribbon-like leaves.

Scientists wanted to use the same method to send medicine into patients' bodies. The result was a new medical sponge. The sponge is made of a jelly that comes from seaweed.

First, doctors fill the sponge with medicine. Then they shrink the sponge so it is very small. They place the sponge inside a needle. This allows them to inject it into a part of the patient's body. Once there, the sponge expands. It slowly releases the medicine. Then it dissolves.

The sponge was first developed in 2012. However, it could be a while before doctors can use the tool. As of 2018, scientists were still testing it.

One porcupine quill has approximately 700 to 800 spikes on its end.

Scientists are also working on a new kind of staple. Doctors use staples to hold skin in place after surgery. Staples have two prongs that pierce the top layers of the skin. The new staples are based on porcupine quills. A porcupine quill has sharp spikes at its end. One scientist tested a quill by poking it into his skin.

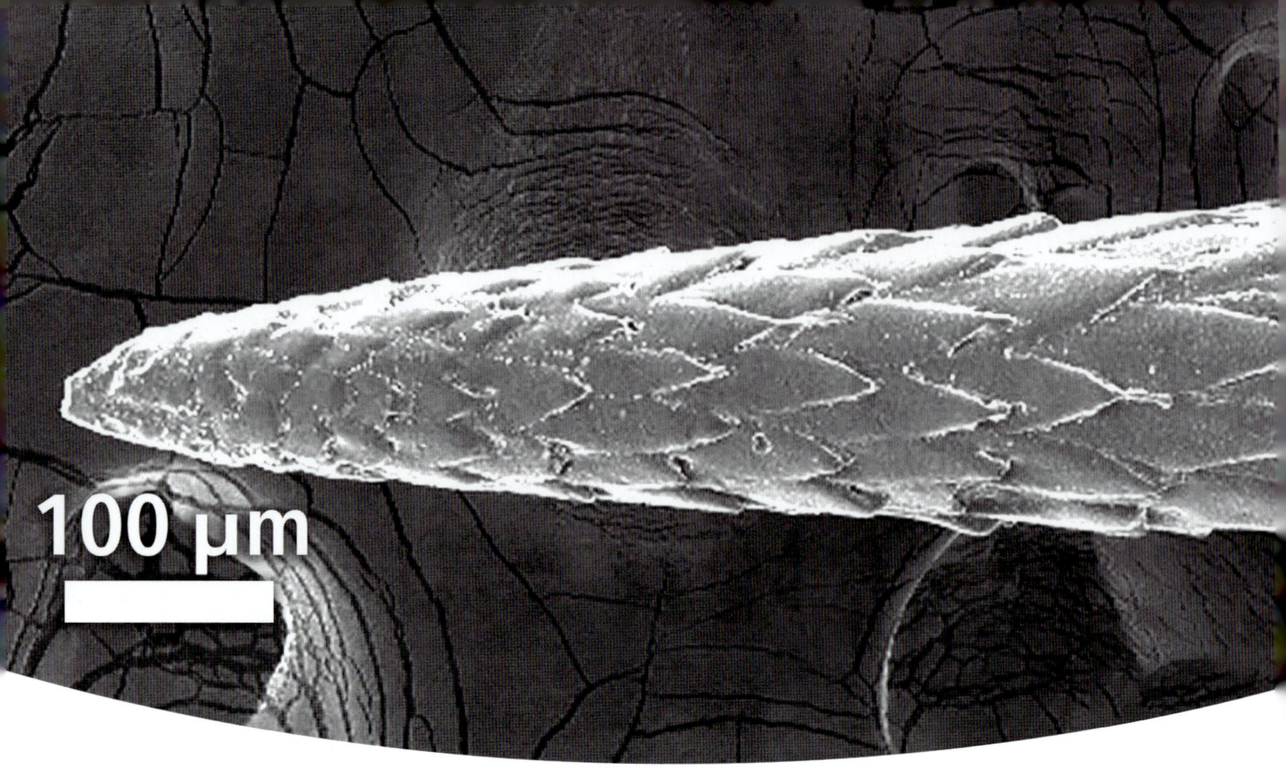

Scientists made a copy of a porcupine quill to use as a staple. It has spikes as small as 100 micrometers (µm).

The quill made a small, clean hole. The spikes helped the quill go in easily.

Most surgical staples make large holes in the skin. This means more **bacteria** can enter the wound. The bacteria often cause infection. Similar to a quill, the new staples would have spikes. The spikes would allow the staple to make small holes. Infection would be less likely. The spikes would also keep the staple in place. Once the staple was no longer needed, it would dissolve inside the body. The staples are still being tested. But one day, they could help many patients in hospitals.

The world is full of fascinating animals and plants. As scientists study them, they continue to find new ideas for medical technology. Such technology does more than copy nature. It takes what works in nature and then builds upon it. In this way, the technology leaves a lasting mark on the future of medicine.

FOCUS ON

MEDICAL TECHNOLOGY INSPIRED BY NATURE

Write your answers on a separate piece of paper.

1. Write a paragraph that summarizes the technologies mentioned in Chapter 2.
2. If you were a designer of medical technology, what would you create? Which animal or plant might inspire you?
3. Which animal inspired the sugar-coated vaccine?
   - A. gecko
   - B. jellyfish
   - C. tardigrade
4. What would happen if the seaweed-inspired medical sponge did not expand properly?
   - A. The doctor would not be able to insert it into the patient's body.
   - B. The medicine would not release properly.
   - C. The doctor would not be able to fill it with medicine.

Answer key on page 32.

GLOSSARY

bacteria
Single-celled living things. They can be useful or harmful.

cancer cells
Abnormal cells that divide and grow in the body.

compound
A substance that is made by combining two or more chemical elements.

DNA
The genetic material in the cells of living organisms.

dormant
Alive but not active, as if in a deep sleep.

expire
To reach the end of the time when something is useful.

extinct
No longer living on Earth.

microchip
A small piece of hardware that has tiny electrical circuits.

tissue
A group of similar cells that have a certain job or function.

vaccine
A substance that prevents a person from getting a disease.

TO LEARN MORE

BOOKS

Becker, Helaine. *Zoobots: Wild Robots Inspired by Real Animals*. Tonawanda, NY: Kids Can Press, 2014.

Gregory, Josh. *From Butterfly Wings to . . . Display Technology*. Ann Arbor, MI: Cherry Lake Publishing, 2014.

Mara, Wil. *From Gecko Feet to . . . Adhesive Tape*. Ann Arbor, MI: Cherry Lake Publishing, 2014.

NOTE TO EDUCATORS

Visit **www.focusreaders.com** to find lesson plans, activities, links, and other resources related to this title.

INDEX

Answer Key: 1. Answers will vary; **2.** Answers will vary; **3.** C; **4.** B

HELPING *Women* SUCCEED IN BUSINESS

Everything You Need to
Know to Achieve Your Career Goals

Nina Baldwin

AVIVA PUBLISHING
New York

HELPING WOMEN SUCCEED IN BUSINESS

Everything You Need to Know to Achieve Your Career Goals

Nina Baldwin
www.HelpingWomenSucceedinBusiness.com

Published by:
Aviva Publishing
Lake Placid, NY
518-523-1320
www.avivapubs.com

ISBN: 978-1-938686-52-8

Library of Congress Control Number: 2013907488

Editor: Tyler Tichelaar

Cover & Interior Design: Fusion Creative Works,
www.fusioncw.com

First Edition

For additional copies visit:
www.HelpingWomenSucceedinBusiness.com